MW00803721

Daddy Poems

Selected by **John Micklos, Jr.**

Illustrated by **Robert Casilla**
with a foreword by **Jim Trelease**

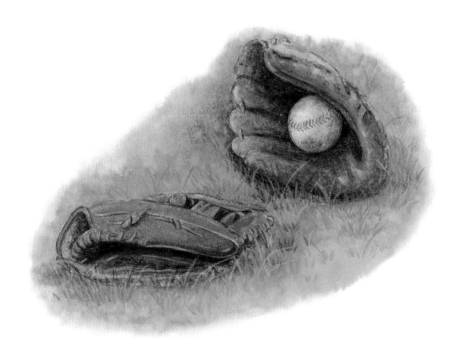

Wordsong
Boyds Mills Press

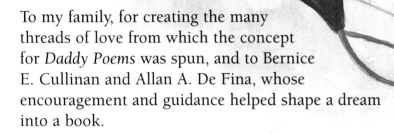

To my family, for creating the many
threads of love from which the concept
for *Daddy Poems* was spun, and to Bernice
E. Cullinan and Allan A. De Fina, whose
encouragement and guidance helped shape a dream
into a book.

—J. M., Jr.

To my children, Robert, Jr. and Emily, who modeled for the book.
And Carmen, my wife.

—R. C.

Published by Wordsong
Boyds Mills Press, Inc.
A Highlights Company
815 Church Street
Honesdale, Pennsylvania 18431
Printed in China

U.S. Cataloging-in-Publication Data
   (Library of Congress Standards)

Micklos, John.
      Daddy poems / compiled by John Micklos Jr. ; illustrated by Robert
Casilla. 1st ed.
[32]p. : col. ill. ;   cm.
Summary: Poems in celebration of fatherhood.
ISBN 1-56397-735-4 hc   1-56397-870-9 pbk
1. Fathers — Juvenile poetry. 2. Children's poetry, American. [1.
Fathers — Poetry. 2. American poetry.] I. Casilla, Robert, ill. II.
Title.
811.54 —dc21   2000   AC   CIP
99-63735

First edition, 2000
The text of this book is set in 15-point Berkeley.

10 9 8 7 6 5 4 3 2 1 hc
10 9 8 7 6 5 4 3 2 1 pbk

Table of Contents

Foreword

by Jim Trelease

I don't think it's any news to any adult reader that fatherhood has not exactly been "celebrated" in the headlines in recent years. Some of that has been our own fault, but lost in the "bad news" have been the unsung millions of dads who not only support their kids, but also cherish and cheer, admonish and cajole, and tease and teach them. These are the ones who have been "keeping their promises" for years.

Lost also in the bleakness of the headlines is that "busy fathers" is not a new phenomenon. At the beginning of the 20th century, fathers worked 14-hour days in the fields and factories, dragging themselves home at dusk. Even among those dog-tired men, there were those who knew their day had not ended until they had played with their children. No, they were not all the fathers, maybe not even the majority, but there were some. And because of them, their children eventually became better parents themselves.

It was that cycle the Greek philosopher referred to when he said, "When you affect the life of a child, you affect not only today and tomorrow, but eternity."

It is especially appropriate that this collection is meant to be read to children by their dads. Outside of hugging a child, few things bring parent and child as close together physically, emotionally, and intellectually as reading. We've all heard the expression "giving a child a piece of our mind," and when we read to them we do just that—but in a far gentler fashion.

So, dads, curl up with your family and enjoy this celebration of those timeless hugs and squeezes, games and stories, chats and piggybacks that add up to this one-of-a-kind guy called "Dad."

—Jim Trelease
Author, *The Read-Aloud Handbook*

A Poem for Me

It was still dark when I woke up
and stumbled out of bed,
sleepily searching for my slippers
on my way to the bathroom.

Light trickled out beneath the door
of the family room.
I turned the doorknob quietly
and peeked inside.

There sat Dad at his writing desk,
staring at a piece of paper,
deep in thought.
I went to him.

"What are you doing?" I asked.
"Writing a poem," he said.
"For you."
He took me in his lap.

"May I read it?" I asked,
peeking at the paper.
"Not yet," he said, lifting me back down.
"It's not quite done yet."

But now it is.

John Micklos, Jr.

6

7

Daddy

When Daddy shaves and lets me stand and look,
I like it better than a picture book.
He pulls such lovely faces all the time
Like funny people in a pantomime.

Rose Fyleman

Porcupine Pa

Whenever Pa neglects to shave
He goes around and kisses
Us loved ones, scratching with his chin—
We duck and hope he misses.

Maybe I lucked out in a way
To get a loving pater,
And yet—who likes to feel like cheese
That's up against a grater?

X. J. Kennedy

8

Piggyback Dad

I don't want the ride to end,
I hug your back.
We ride again
Around the table
Past the chair
Through the kitchen
Up the stairs.
I laugh until I cannot see,
I laugh because you're galloping
As if we are a horse and rider
(We ride crazy-wild together!),
And soon it isn't you and me,
But only one horse—
That is *we*.
Closer than the closest we are then,
I hold you tight
Right to the end.

Deborah Chandra

Kitchen Waltz

My small bare feet
spoon his shoes,
sideways, slide,
one step, two—
and here we go along the floor,
toe-piggybacking *three*
and four,
around my dancing
giant goes,
trailing me on leather soles,
five steps,
six,
spin and dip,
dancing Daddy please don't quit;
the world is big but *I* belong
to Daddy's
kitchen waltzing song.

Rebecca Kai Dotlich

10

Father's Magic

Hundreds of starlings
landed on my trees.
"Come look," my father said.
He clapped his hands,
once, twice,
and all the starlings
flew away.

Emanuel di Pasquale

from **Night Driving**

We walk outside.
Suddenly, I see giant peaks,
sharp as bear's teeth,
that push into the sky.

"Look, Dad, the mountains."
I feel his hand on my shoulder,
and way up high,
I see snow sparkling in the light.

John Coy

12

from *Calling the Doves*

At noon time,
on a lunch break from driving the tractor,
my father made bird calls.

He would put his hands up to his mouth
and whistle deeply as if he had a tiny clarinet
inside the palms of his hands.

"This is how a dove sings," my father would say.

Sooner or later a real dove would fly in
and perch itself on a nearby tree.

Juan Felipe Herrera

13

First Baseball Glove

"Stee-rike," George yells.
I pitch the tennis ball;
George catches.
"Baw" he says just
like he's heard
the umpires say in Yankee Stadium.

Dad comes downstairs
from our city apartment
and watches for a minute
while we throw the tennis ball.
"Come with me," he says.

"We're goin' to Sears."
He sounds excited.
He walks fast
like he's going places
and he can't wait to get there.

We go straight past toys to sports.
"Here's a catcher's mitt, George.
You're the catcher."
"Don, here's a fielder's mitt.
Try it on; see how it fits."

We race home and toss a ball
back and forth;
we yell and shout,
make the calls
with a hard baseball,
real leather mitts;
we race upstairs
to show them to Mother.

Her eyes grow dark,
she breathes deeply,
her mouth open
like she's trying to find words,
   any words, and she looks
      straight at Dad.

14

"You didn't spend
the food money, did you?"
Dad looks at the floor
like he's had a hard life.
"Time the boys had gloves."

"You boys go downstairs
while we talk," Mom says.
We play one more game
on the sidewalk,
whipping the ball,
feeling the sting
smart in the pocket.

Donald Graves

15

Pretty

Pretty.
That's what Daddy
says I am
whenever he comes
to get me.
I love him
and I'm glad
he's gonna come today.

Oh, I wish he'd hurry up!

Nikki Grimes

16

My Father

My father doesn't live with us.
It doesn't help to make a fuss;
But still I feel unhappy, plus
    I miss him.

My father doesn't live with me.
He's got another family;
He moved away when I was three.
    I miss him.

I'm always happy on the day
He visits and we talk and play;
But after he has gone away
    I miss him.

Mary Ann Hoberman

My José

When he sees friends come home with me
he always says hello,
and if they're new friends
I'm supposed to tell their names and his name.
The problem is I don't know what to call him.

Stepfather is strange.

He's not my dad.

Mister is an uptight word.

I try to get outdoors to play
before he notices,
but if I can't I finally just say,

Hey guys, this is my José.

Martha S. Robinson

Will I Be Big?

Someday
    Will I be big like you, Daddy?

Yes, honey, but not yet.

Will I have a stubbly chin
    that prickles when
    people kiss me?

Yes, honey, but not yet.

Will my arms be long
—so long I could
    wrap up three kids
    with them?

Yes, honey, but not yet.

Will my hands be so big
    that I could hide
    a little kid's hand inside
    and you can't even see
    a pinky fingernail?

Yes, honey, but not yet.

And Daddy,
When I'm big
    will my eyes
    look kinda watery
    and red around the edges
when my little boy
    asks me questions?

Yes, honey,

    but, oh,

        not yet.

Jane Medina

Dad

I sometimes wish
he'd squeeze me
the way he used to do
when I was little.
I wish he'd
pick me up and swing me in the air
and whoosh me by my ankles
onto my bed
like he did when I was small.
He doesn't seem to tickle me
that much these days, either.
I almost wish he'd rub his
beard against my cheeks, like before,
even though I used to complain
that it hurt.
But he doesn't do these things anymore.

Every once in a while, though,
he messes my hair
and pokes me in my ribs.
He smiles at me and I smile back.
I love my Dad
and I know he loves me.

Allan A. De Fina

20

Daddy Hugs

Sometimes Dad gives gentle hugs,
wraps both his arms around me—
cuddly, warm, and special hugs
that with his love surround me.

Sometimes Dad gives squeezy hugs
that make me laugh and smile—
strong and warm and special hugs
that last a long, long while.

My favorite hugs are family hugs
when Dad hugs Mom *and* me—
great big all-together hugs
with love enough for three!

John Micklos, Jr.

Happy

When my daddy comes home
And wants to see
Just me,
I'm happy!
When we find his special chair
And he smooths my messy hair,
I'm happy!
Sometimes he tells me silly stories
Or says funny words over and over
And then tickles me.
We sing songs, make oogly faces
Or he chases me real fast.
When my daddy comes right home
And wants to see
Just me,
I'm happy!

Stacy Jo Crossen
Natalie Anne Covell

My Daddy Is a Cool Dude

When my daddy comes in from work
at night
he always say
"Hey man, gimme five"
and I lay it on him
and he smiles.

My daddy sure is a cool dude.

Karama Fufuka

Our Daily Bread

Nine P.M. we close the store,
wash the counter, mop the floor.

Ten P.M. we finally eat.
Father pulls up a milk crate seat

to the table and we pray
Thank you for this crazy day.

Janet S. Wong

23

Bath Time

Bath time is my favorite time.
Dad puts me in the tub.
He helps me lather up with soap
And then we start to scrub.

We scrub my face and ears and neck
And then we wash my hair.
We scrub my back and legs and feet.
We scrub me here and there!

When I'm all clean it's time to play.
Dad puts my tub toys in:
My ducky and my fleet of boats,
And then the fun begins.

I like to dive beneath the suds,
Swim laps and splash some more.
Dad thinks it's all quite funny 'til
Waves splash out on the floor.

Then playtime ends; Dad dries me off.
I'm clean as I can get.
By the time my bath is over, though,
Everything is wet!

John Micklos, Jr.

24

Bedtime Ritual

I need another cookie, Dad.
I need another drink.
I need another visit
To the bathroom, I think.

I need another story, please.
I need another song.
I need to sit here in your lap
So I can sing along.

I need my favorite teddy bear.
I need to hold it tight.
I need for you to please turn on
My little red night-light.

I need another good-night kiss.
Then I can go to bed.
I love you, Dad. Good night. Good night.
Now I'll lay down my head.

John Micklos, Jr.

Hippity Hop to Bed

O it's hippity hop to bed!
I'd rather sit up instead.
But when father says "must,"
There's nothing but just
Go hippity hop to bed.

Leroy F. Jackson

Bedtime

"Read me a story,
Please read me to sleep."
"What kind of story, my love?"
"Of raindrops and rainbows
And furry soft kittens
And ponies and gentle white doves."

"Read me a story,
Please read me to sleep."
"What kind of story, my sweet?"
"Of magical castles
And harps that can sing
And gypsies who dance in the street."

"Read me a story,
Please read me to sleep."
"What kind of story, my pet?"
"Of pirates and treasure
And ships in the night
And mermaids who escape from a net."

"Read me a story,
Please read me to sleep."
"What kind of story, my child?"
"Of mountains and meadows
And bubbling brooks
And stallions who run free and wild."

"Read me a story,
Please read me to sleep."
"What kind of story, my dear?"
"Read any story
And I'll go to sleep,
As long as I know you are near."

David L. Harrison

Index of Authors

Index of First Lines

Biographical Notes About the Poets

Deborah Chandra, a former elementary school teacher, has written several poetry and story poem books for children. In 1995 she received the *Lee Bennett Hopkins Promising Poet Award* from the International Reading Association.

Stacy Jo Crossen and **Natalie Anne Covell** collaborated on many poems, including the one in this book, which appeared in their book *Me Is How I Feel*.

John Coy's contribution to *Daddy Poems* comes from his book *Night Driving*, a poignant prose description of a father and son's journey together through the night in the family car.

Allan A. De Fina has more than 20 years of teaching experience and currently teaches at New Jersey City University. He has published articles and books about education, as well as the children's poetry book *When a City Leans Against the Sky*.

Emanuel di Pasquale's poems have appeared in several children's magazines and in many anthologies. His poems for adults have appeared in national magazines, newspapers, and journals.

Rebecca Kai Dotlich's poems have appeared in many children's magazines and in several anthologies. Her books for children include the poetry books *Sweet Dreams of the Wild* and *Lemonade Sun and Other Summer Poems*.

Karama Fufuka has written many poems and stories for children. Her contribution to *Daddy Poems* comes from her book *My Daddy Is a Cool Dude*, which was illustrated by her husband, Mahiri Fufuka.

Rose Fyleman was a noted English writer for children. Her many works include plays, poems, and nursery rhymes, and she had a special interest in fairies.

Donald Graves is a noted educator and author of professional books for teachers. He also writes poetry for children, and his contribution to *Daddy Poems* comes from his book *Baseball, Snakes, and Summer Squash: Poems About Growing Up*.

Nikki Grimes has published poems, articles, essays, editorials, and photographs in many national markets. She has written several books for young people, including *Something on My Mind*.

David L. Harrison is the author of several popular poetry and picture books for children. His works include *Somebody Catch My Homework* and *When Cows Come Home*.

Juan Felipe Herrera is a poet, actor, musician, and professor. He is the author of several poetry books, and his contribution to *Daddy Poems* is excerpted from his award-winning book *Calling the Doves*.

Mary Ann Hoberman is the author of many books for children. Her works include the award-winning book *A House Is a House for Me* and *Fathers, Mothers, Sisters, Brothers: A Collection of Family Poems*.

Leroy F. Jackson's poetry in the early 1900s included many light-hearted, family-oriented verses such as "Hippity Hop to Bed," which appeared in his book *The Peter Patter Book*.

X. J. Kennedy is a noted writer and anthologist. In addition to writing textbooks, novels, and poetry books for children, he has also written poetry for adults.

Jane Medina is a new poet whose writings reflect the love she has developed for children, poetry, and education in her 21 years as an elementary school teacher.

John Micklos, Jr. has been an education writer and editor for more than 20 years. He has written materials for a wide range of adult and children's publications. *Daddy Poems* is his second children's book.

Martha S. Robinson was a professor of law emeritus at Loyola Law School in Los Angeles, California. She was also the author of *The Zoo at Night*, a children's picture book.

Janet S. Wong practiced law for a number of years before deciding to devote her time to writing. Her works include the children's poetry books *A Suitcase of Seaweed and Other Poems* and *Good Luck Gold and Other Poems*.

John Micklos, Jr.

has written for national publications ranging from *Cobblestone* to *Modern Bride* and is the author of the book *Leonard Nimoy: A Star's Trek*. He is editor-in-chief of *Reading Today*, the membership newspaper of the International Reading Association. He has served as president of EdPress, the Association of Educational Publishers. He lives in Newark, Delaware with his wife, Debbie, and his two children, Amy and John.

Robert Casilla

works at home in his studio in Yonkers, NY. His wife Carmen, and his children, Robert, Jr., and Emily, often are models for his illustrations. His work has appeared in *The New York Times*, *The Daily News*, *Black Enterprise*, and other magazines. In addition to illustrating books for children, Casilla also has illustrated postage stamps for independent countries such as Grenada and Sierra Leone.

Acknowledgments

"Piggyback Dad," from *Balloons and Other Poems* by Deborah Chandra. Copyright © 1990 by Deborah Chandra. Reprinted by permission of Farrar, Straus & Giroux, Inc.

Excerpt from *Night Driving* by John Coy, © 1996 by John Coy. Reprinted by permission of Henry Holt and Company, Inc. and John Coy.

"Happy," from *Me Is How I Feel: Poems* by Stacy Jo Crossen and Natalie Anne Covell. Copyright © 1970 by A. Harris Stone, Stacy Crossen, Natalie Covell, Victoria deLarrea. Used by permission of Dutton Signet, a division of Penguin Books USA, Inc.

"Dad," by Allan A. De Fina. Copyright © 1997. Original poem.

"Father's Magic," by Emanuel di Pasquale. From *Poems for Fathers*, selected by Myra Cohn Livingston and published by Holiday House, 1989. Copyright © 1989 by Emanuel di Pasquale.

"Kitchen Waltz," by Rebecca Kai Dotlich. Original poem. Copyright © 1999 by Rebecca Kai Dotlich. Reprinted by permission of Curtis Brown, Ltd.

"My Daddy Is a Cool Dude," from *My Daddy Is a Cool Dude and Other Poems* by Karama Fufuka. Copyright © 1975 by Karama Fufuka. Used by permission of Dial Books for Young Readers, a division of Penguin Books USA, Inc.

"Daddy," by Rose Fyleman. Found on p. 165 of *Sing a Song of Seasons*, selected by Sara and John Brewton and published by Macmillan Press, 1955. Reprinted with permission from *Fairies and Friends* by Rose Fyleman. Copyright © 1926 by Doubleday. Public Domain.

"First Baseball Glove," by Donald Graves. From *Baseball, Snakes, and Summer Squash: Poems About Growing Up*. Copyright © 1996 by Donald Graves. Published by Boyds Mills Press, Inc. Reprinted by permission.

"Pretty," from *Something on My Mind* by Nikki Grimes. Copyright © 1978 by Nikki Grimes. Used by permission of Dial Books for Young Readers, a division of Penguin Books USA, Inc.

"Bedtime," from *The Boy Who Counted Stars*, by David L. Harrison. Text copyright ©1994 by David L. Harrison. Published by Boyds Mills Press, Inc. Reprinted by permission.

Excerpt from *Calling the Doves* by Juan Felipe Herrera. Reprinted with permission of the publisher, Children's Book Press, San Francisco, CA. Story copyright © 1995 by Juan Felipe Herrera.

"My Father," by Mary Ann Hoberman. From *Fathers, Mothers, Sisters, Brothers* by Mary Ann Hoberman. Text copyright © 1991 by Mary Ann Hoberman. By permission of Little, Brown and Company.

"Hippity Hop to Bed," by Leroy F. Jackson. Found on p. 100 of *Time for Poetry* (3rd Ed.), selected by May Hill Arbuthnot and published by Scott Foresman, 1968. Reprinted by permission from *The Peter Patter Book* by Leroy F. Jackson, published by Rand McNally & Co., 1918. Public Domain.

"Porcupine Pa," by X. J. Kennedy. From *The Forgetful Wishing Well* by X. J. Kennedy, published by Margaret K. McElderry Books, copyright © 1985.

"Will I Be Big?" by Jane Medina. Copyright © 1998. Original poem.

"A Poem for Me," "Bath Time," "Bedtime Ritual," and "Daddy Hugs," by John Micklos, Jr. Copyright © 1998. Original poems.

"My José," by Martha S. Robinson. From *Poems for Fathers*, selected by Myra Cohn Livingston, and published by Holiday House, 1989. Copyright © 1989 by Martha S. Robinson.

"Our Daily Bread," by Janet S. Wong. Reprinted with the permission of Margaret K. McElderry Books, an imprint of Simon & Schuster Children's Publishing Division, from *A Suitcase of Seaweed and Other Poems* by Janet S. Wong. Copyright © 1996 by Janet S. Wong.

Every effort has been made to trace the ownership of each poem included in *Daddy Poems*. If any errors or omissions have occurred, corrections will be made in subsequent printings, provided the publisher is notified of their existence. We gratefully acknowledge those who granted permission to use the poems that appear in this book.

J
811.008
D

Daddy poems.

DATE			